Never Ask a Bear

Never Ask a Bear

By
Louise Bonnett-Rampersaud

Illustrated by
Doris Barrette

HarperCollins *Publishers*

To all the "bears" in my life who
make huge messes! Love you all!
—L.B.-R.

For Zachari
—D.B.

Never Ask a Bear
Text copyright © 2009 by Louise Bonnett-Rampersaud
Illustrations copyright © 2009 by Doris Barrette
Manufactured in China. All rights reserved. No part of this book may be used or reproduced
in any manner whatsoever without written permission except in the case of brief quotations
embodied in critical articles and reviews. For information address HarperCollins Children's
Books, a division of HarperCollins Publishers, 10 East 53rd Street, New York, NY 10022.
www.harpercollinschildrens.com

Library of Congress Cataloging-in-Publication Data
Bonnett-Rampersaud, Louise. Never ask a bear / by Louise Bonnett-Rampersaud ; illustrated
by Doris Barrette. — 1st ed. p. cm. Summary: Ten rhyming rules explain why bears do not
make good playmates. ISBN 978-0-06-112876-9 (trade bdg.) ISBN 978-0-06-112878-3
(lib. bdg.) [1. Stories in rhyme. 2. Bears—Fiction. 3. Humorous stories.] I. Barrette,
Doris, ill. II. Title. PZ8.3.B63Ne 2009 2008022596 [E]—dc22 CIP AC

Design by Stephanie Bart-Horvath

09 10 11 12 13 SCP 10 9 8 7 6 5 4 3 2 1 ❖ First Edition

If you're having a bear over to play,

There are things you should know,

There are things you should say.

I'll tell you the rules—

Numbers one up through ten.

Then have Mom or Dad read them . . .

Again . . . and again!

Rule #1

NEVER ask a bear
to close your front door.

Because . . .

He'll slam it

And bang it

And push it real hard.

And then your front door

Will end up in your yard!

Rule #2

DON'T ask a bear
to "Please take a seat."

Because . . .

He'll crunch it

And munch it

And nibble and eat,

And your mom's favorite chair

Will end up as a treat!

Rule #3

DON'T ever let a bear know
you have a little brother or sister.

Because . . .

He'll chase them

And race them

And scare them and roar,

'Til the poor little kid

Is in tears on the floor.

Rule #4

NEVER, ever play dress up with a bear.

Because . . .

He'll squeeze into tutus

And stockings

And things,

And he'll crash all about

As he dances and sings.

Rule #5

DON'T play ball outside with a bear.

Because . . .

He'll bounce it

And kick it

And throw it real hard,

'Til your brand-new red ball's

In your neighbor's backyard.

Rule #6

NEVER ask a bear
if he's thirsty.

Because . . .

He won't want a cup

Or a mug

For his drink.

No! He'll slurp and he'll gulp

From your mom's kitchen sink!

Rule #7

NEVER paint when you have a
bear over to play.

Because...

He'll paint puppies

And cats and

Baby bears, too.

And all without paper . . .

As bears like to do!

Rule #8

NEVER let a bear help you
bake cookies.

Because...

He'll mix

And he'll splatter

The batter and dough.

And he'll whip it about

With his paws, don't you know!

Rule #9

DON'T ever let a bear take a bath.

Because . . .

He'll splish

And he'll splash

All the water galore,

'Til there's none in the bath

And a lot on the floor!

Rule #10

NEVER play hide-and-seek
with a bear.

He'll hide

And you'll count

And you'll find him all right.

But he'll get himself stuck

For the whole day and night!

So

I've told you the rules

As I said I would do.

But a piece of advice

Just between me and you—

Have Katie

Or Freddy

Or Julie

Or Stu

Come over to play

When you're with . . .

You-know-who.

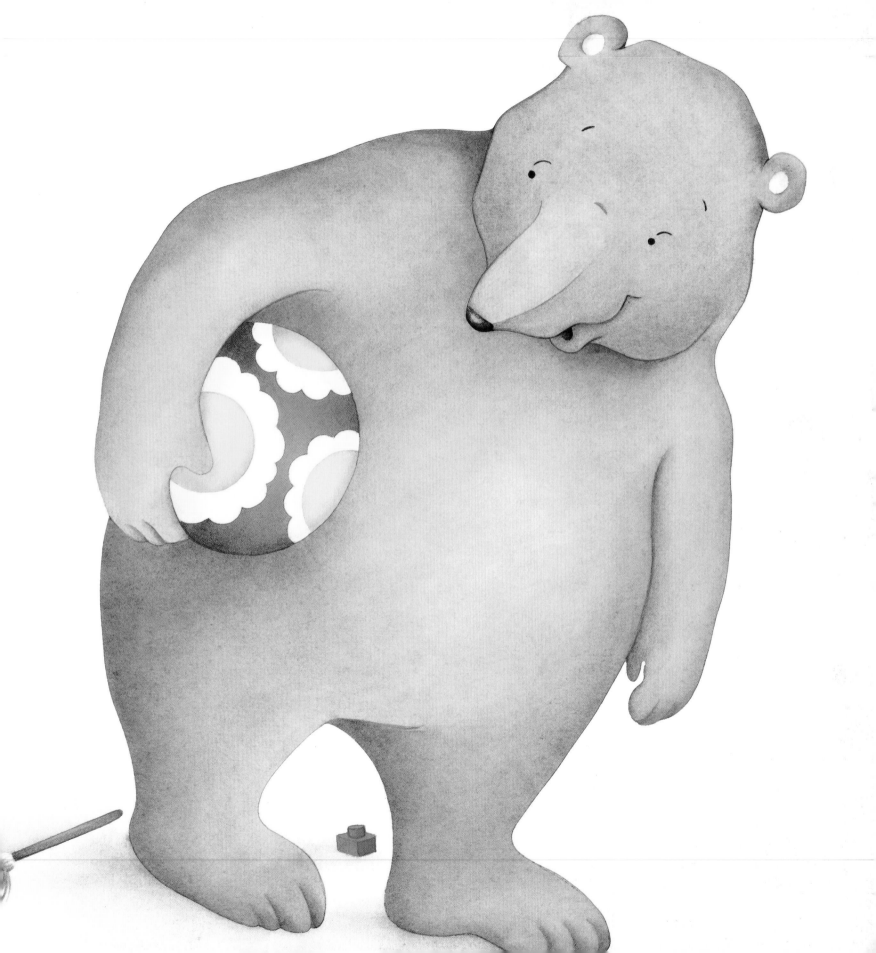